Lily Finds a Friend

There was something furry lying under one of the bushes. It was almost hidden under all the leaves, but Lily had spotted it.

"What's that?" Lily woofed to herself.

She dropped down onto her tummy and crawled toward the furry thing. Gently, she reached out a paw to touch it. . . .

Lily Finds a Friend

Lily Finds a Friend

by Jenny Dale

illustrated by Susan Hellard

SCHOLASTIC INC.

New York   Toronto   London   Auckland   Sydney
Mexico City   New Delhi   Hong Kong   Buenos Aires

ISBN 0-439-79123-5

Text copyright © 2001 by Working Partners Limited
Illustrations copyright © 2001 by Susan Hellard

All rights reserved. Published by Scholastic Inc., 557 Broadway, New York, NY 10012, by arrangement with Macmillan Children's Books, London, England. JENNY DALE'S PUPPY TALES is a trademark of Working Partners Limited. SCHOLASTIC and associated logos are trademarks and/or registered trademarks of Scholastic Inc.

12 11 10 9 8 7   7 8 9 10 11/0

Printed in the U.S.A.
First printing, January 2006

Chapter One

"I'm bored!" Lily woofed. She slumped down at the top of the stairs. "Bored, bored, bored!"

Jack, Lily's owner, had gone to school, and Mrs. Harper, Jack's mom, was at work. Mr. Harper was at home today, but he was busy putting up a shelf in the living room. He'd been sawing and hammering all morning, and he'd shooed Lily out of the room and shut the door. He'd said that Lily was getting under his feet.

"What nerve!" Lily yapped. She put her nose between her paws and stared gloomily down the stairs. "I was only trying to help. It wasn't *my* fault that Mr. Harper dropped the hammer on his toe."

The brown-and-white puppy looked around for something to do. Then she spotted her little rubber ball lying on Jack's bedroom floor. "Oh, great!" Lily yapped, cheering up a bit. "I can play my favorite game."

Lily trotted into Jack's bedroom to get the ball and carried it to the

top of the stairs in her mouth.
Then she let it go.

THUD! THUD! THUD! The ball
bounced loudly down the stairs,
with Lily racing after it. She
caught it at the bottom, and then
dashed back up the stairs again.

THUD! THUD! THUD! Lily ran
down the stairs after the ball

again, just as Mr. Harper flung open the living-room door.

"Lily!" he called crossly. "Stop making all that noise!"

"Huh!" Lily sniffed. "I'm not the one making all the noise — you are."

Mr. Harper went back into the living room, but this time he left the door open. Lily immediately trotted after him.

She saw that Jack's dad had put up the shelf and was stacking lots of books on it. Lily wagged her tail. Maybe Mr. Harper would play with her now that he'd finished his work.

But suddenly, there was a loud, cracking noise. The shelf tilted, and one end of it came right off the wall. All the books slid off and landed with a crash on the floor.

"Oh, no!" Jack's dad groaned.

"Never mind, Mr. Harper," Lily woofed, rubbing her head on his shin. "But you better get it fixed, or you're going to be in big trouble with Mrs. Harper when she gets home."

Lily left Jack's dad picking up the books, and trotted into the kitchen. There was no way Mr. Harper was going to have time to play with her now!

She decided to go outside, to see if her friend Charlie was at home. Charlie lived next door with Sally and her family. Sally was Jack's friend.

Lily nosed her way through her dog flap and bounded out into the yard. "Charlie!" she barked loudly. "Come and play with me. I'm bored." Then she pricked up her ears, waiting for Charlie's answering bark from the other side of the fence.

There was no reply. *Charlie must have gone out with Sally's mom,* Lily thought gloomily. None of her friends were at home today. Lily seemed to be the only one with nothing to do.

Suddenly, Lily had an idea. Her brown eyes lit up. "I could find a *new* friend," she woofed, her tail wagging like crazy. "*Then* I'll have someone to play with."

Lily was so excited by her idea

that she ran around in circles for a while, trying to catch her tail. Then she sat down, panting, and looked around the yard. Where should she start?

She knew that Jack had asked his mom and dad to make sure there was no way Lily could escape from the yard. The puppy had gotten lost a few times before, and Jack was very worried that it might happen again.

"I promise I won't get lost *this* time, though, Jack!" Lily woofed softly as she sniffed her way along the fence, hoping to find a hole she could squeeze through.

But Jack's mom and dad had made sure there were no gaps in the fence at all. Not even a small one. There was simply no way out.

Lily sat down on the grass, her ears drooping. "I need someone to play with," she whimpered sadly.

Suddenly, she spotted something moving under a big bush at the back of the yard. She jumped up, her sturdy little body quivering. Then she dashed over to investigate.

It was a small, green creature with big, bulging eyes. It hopped out in front of her, and gave a loud *CROAK*.

"Hello!" Lily panted excitedly. "Will you be my friend?" And she rushed forward to give the creature a big, wet lick.

The creature backed away in
alarm. It croaked even louder,
then hopped quickly out of sight.

Lily dived into the bushes after
it. She hadn't explored this end of
the yard much because it was
very overgrown. It was so damp
and dark, Lily had always felt a
little scared. But now she was

determined to find her new friend again.

What was that, half hidden behind that big bush? Lily forgot her chase. She could see a hole in the fence!

Chapter Two

Lily could hardly believe her luck. First of all, though, she had to squeeze behind the bush to get a good look at the hole.

It wasn't easy. The bush was *very* big and bushy indeed. Lily puffed and panted, her little pink tongue hanging out, before she managed to fight her way through.

Feeling excited, Lily peered through the hole, her tail wagging madly. She was looking into a huge, overgrown yard. It was much bigger than hers, with tall trees surrounding it on every side and a lawn in the middle. At the far end of the yard stood a big, old house.

"Hurrah!" Lily barked happily. "This looks wonderful. I hope the people who live here like dogs. I might find a new friend."

Lily began to climb eagerly through the hole. She was halfway through, when suddenly she stopped. Jack's voice had just popped into her head. *Don't wander off and get lost AGAIN, Lily,* he was saying anxiously.

Lily's tail stopped wagging while she thought about this. "But I'm not going to get lost, am I?" she woofed to herself. "I'm only going to be on the other side of this hole. I can find my way back into our yard any time I want."

Her tail started wagging again, and she continued scrambling through the hole. It was a bit of a struggle to get her chubby little bottom through, but Lily managed it. Then she trotted out onto the lawn and gazed around. The yard seemed even bigger now that she was actually in it.

Lily started toward the house, her black nose to the ground. There were so many exciting new smells to investigate that she kept veering off into the flower borders and under the bushes. She could smell the scents of people, as well as lots of different animals.

Suddenly, a squirrel darted out of a thick patch of undergrowth and ran across the lawn.

Lily's eyes lit up. "Hello," she woofed, dashing after it. "Be my friend!"

But the squirrel didn't seem very friendly at all. It raced up the trunk of the nearest tree and disappeared among the leaves.

A moment or two later, Lily had to jump out of the way when an acorn crashed to the ground very close to her. "How rude!" she yapped, disappointed. "Never mind, I'm sure the people who live here will be a lot nicer." And she bounded across the grass toward the house.

There were some steps leading up to a patio, and beyond it were some glass doors into the house. Lily panted with excitement as she trotted up the steps and dashed over to the windows. Tail wagging madly, she peered hopefully inside.

An old man was sitting in an armchair in the large living room, watching TV. He had a tray on his lap with a cup of tea and a big slice of apple pie.

Lily licked her lips. She was feeling a little hungry. "Hello!" she woofed, tapping on the glass with her paw. "I'm Lily, and I *love* pie. Will you be my friend?"

The old man didn't look around. He was too busy watching TV, and he couldn't hear Lily because the sound was turned up so high.

"HELLO-O-OO!" Lily howled

more loudly. "PLEASE BE MY FRIEND!"

But the man still didn't notice her. Lily felt very disappointed.

Maybe there's another way into the house, Lily thought determinedly. She had to get inside before all that lovely pie disappeared.

Lily trotted around to the narrow strip of yard at the side of the house. There was another door, but it was firmly shut, and no one came to open it when Lily scratched at it. There was also a tall gate at the end of the yard. Lily guessed it led around to the front of the house. She could hear the cars going up and down the street, although she couldn't see them.

Suddenly, Lily's sturdy little
body stiffened. She raised her
head and sniffed the air, and
her tail began to wag happily.
It was a smell and a voice that
she'd know anywhere!

"Mom, can Sally come over to
play with me tonight?"

It was Jack! He and his mom

and Sally were walking up the street on the other side of the tall gate, on their way home from school.

Lily was just about to bark a loud greeting when she stopped herself. Oh, dear, Jack wouldn't be very happy if he found her in this strange yard, would he? He didn't like her wandering off on her own.

"I'd better get myself back into our yard — and fast!" Lily yapped anxiously. "I just hope I can make it before Jack gets home."

Lily was about to hurtle back toward the hole when she noticed something very strange.

Chapter Three

There was something furry lying under one of the bushes. It was almost hidden under all the leaves, but Lily had spotted it.

"What's that?" Lily woofed curiously to herself. Even though she knew she should get home right away, she couldn't resist taking a little look. "I'd better be careful, though," she yapped. "It might be dangerous."

So she dropped down onto her tummy and crawled toward the furry thing. Gently, she reached out a paw to touch it. Nothing happened. "*Grr!* Who are you?" she growled. "Are you my friend or not?"

The furry thing still didn't speak or move. Lily wondered if it was another dog. But it didn't smell like one. It didn't smell like a cat, either. What could it be?

She moved even closer and sniffed it all over. Then she took a good look at it. "Oh, it's a teddy bear!" Lily woofed, delighted. She knew what teddy bears were because Jack had an old bear, Herbie, sitting on his pillow. This teddy bear looked even more tattered than Herbie, though. He was very dirty and a little damp and had a frayed red ribbon around his neck.

Lily didn't care. She was thrilled. She'd gone to find herself a new friend — and she'd found one!

"Come on," Lily woofed, picking the bear up gently in her mouth. "I'll look after you from now on!" And the teddy bear seemed to smile at her.

Suddenly, Lily remembered that Jack was on his way home. If she didn't hurry, he might notice that she wasn't there and get upset.

She quickly raced down the

yard, carrying the bear. Now,
where was the hole?

For a moment, Lily couldn't
remember exactly where the hole
was. Her heart beat faster. Then
she spotted it, almost hidden
behind a tall tree. She dashed
over to it.

It was even more of a squeeze
for Lily to get through the hole
with the teddy bear in her mouth.

She pushed and heaved and struggled and panted, until finally the two of them were through. Then Lily pushed her way out from behind the bush.

She was just shaking pieces of twigs and leaves from her furry coat when the back door opened. Jack and Sally came out into the yard.

"There she is," Jack called, waving to her. "Hi, Lil!"

"What's Lily got in her mouth?" Sally laughed, staring at the excited puppy. "It's nearly as big as she is."

Lily raced toward them, tail wagging, and laid the teddy bear down gently on the grass. "This is my new friend," she barked proudly. Then she launched herself at Jack for her usual after-school cuddles.

"Lily, where did you get *that*?" Jack fussed over Lily for a moment or two, then he picked up the bear and examined it. His mom came out of the house. "Mom, look what Lily found," Jack called.

"Oh, dear, it's sort of dirty, isn't it?" Mrs. Harper wrinkled her nose.

"Don't talk about my new friend like that!" Lily yapped indignantly.

"Lily must have found it in the yard," Jack's mom went on. "Maybe it belonged to the people who lived in the house before we moved in."

"The people who lived here

before you *did* have a little baby," Sally agreed. "Maybe it was his teddy bear and they left it behind by accident."

Lily was listening with her head cocked to one side. She'd never thought about who the bear might *really* belong to. Maybe someone was looking for him right this minute. . . .

But if they really wanted the bear, they wouldn't have left him out in the rain and the cold, would they? No, Lily decided, the teddy bear belonged to her from now on.

"Please, Jack, can I play with my new friend?" she barked, pawing impatiently at Jack's legs.

Jack laughed as he bent down to

hand Lily the bear. "There you go, Lil!"

"Oh, Jack," Mrs. Harper said crossly. "It's filthy. If Lily wants to play with it, it'll have to be washed first."

"No way!" Lily growled through her teeth. "My bear's not taking a horrible old bath." And she shot off into the house.

"I don't think you'll get the bear away from her, Mom!" Jack laughed as they followed Lily inside.

He was right. Lily loved her teddy bear so much, she just wouldn't put him down. First, she took her new friend all over the house. She showed him her food and water bowls, then her leash and her toys. Next, she showed him her favorite sleeping spot on the end of Jack's bed. Finally, she took the bear to the living room to meet Mr. Harper, who was still struggling to put up the shelf.

When Jack and Sally went to the corner store to buy some milk for Jack's mom, Lily went, too, with the bear clutched proudly in her mouth. Everyone they passed in the street stopped and smiled when they saw the puppy carrying her teddy bear.

"Lily really loves her bear, doesn't she?" Sally grinned as they walked back from the shop with Lily trotting alongside them.

"I don't think Mom does," Jack replied. "But it looks like Lily's teddy bear is here to stay."

Lily wagged her tail happily. Jack and Sally were right. Now she had a friend to play with while Jack was at school. Lily felt like the luckiest puppy in the whole world!

Chapter Four

"Come on, Teddy!" Lily woofed,
as she climbed through the dog
flap. "Let's go out into the
yard before Mrs. Harper
catches us."

It was the following morning.
Lily had slept curled up on Jack's
bed all night, as she usually did.

But this time, she'd had Teddy lying beside her.

And when Mrs. Harper had popped her head around the door that morning, she'd gasped in dismay. "Oh, Lily! Get that dirty old thing off Jack's bed *at once*!"

"It's okay, Mom." Jack yawned. "I don't mind."

"Well, I do," Mrs. Harper said. "That bear needs a good wash."

"Don't worry, Teddy," Lily barked determinedly. "I'll save you." She grabbed the bear in her teeth and charged out of Jack's bedroom.

Lily clattered down the stairs and into the kitchen. It was Saturday, so when Jack had washed and dressed and eaten his breakfast, he would be taking Lily for an extra-long walk. Until then, Lily was determined to keep her new friend out of Mrs. Harper's clutches.

"Why do people always want to *wash* everything?" Lily whined, as she laid Teddy carefully on the lawn. "Have you ever had a bath, Teddy? It's horrible. All the shampoo gets in your eyes and up your nose, and it makes you sneeze."

It was the beginning of a warm, sunny day. Lily left Teddy lying on the grass sunbathing while she wandered around the yard. She put her nose to the ground, sniffing all the early morning smells.

"Aha!" she barked. "That cat from down the street has been in here again. Do you like cats, Teddy? I don't."

Lily didn't want to leave her new friend on his own for too long, so she soon bounded back across the lawn to him. "What shall we do now, Teddy?" she barked, jumping playfully around the bear. "Oh, I know — I've got a great idea!"

Lily picked Teddy up and headed down the yard toward the hole that led next door. There was more of next door's yard to explore! And maybe another new friend to be found, hidden under a bush, as Teddy was.

Lily had plenty of time, too.

Jack still had to get washed and dressed and eat his breakfast. Then he always watched his favorite cartoon on Saturday mornings before they went out for their walk.

Holding Teddy firmly in her mouth, Lily squeezed through the hole again. She trotted out onto the lawn, just as the squirrel ran down its tree.

"Look, I've got a new friend," Lily barked, forgetting that she had Teddy in her mouth. The bear tumbled out onto the grass. "Oops, sorry, Teddy."

Lily was about to pick Teddy up again when she noticed something very interesting. Because it was a warm and sunny morning, the big glass doors at the back of the house were open.

"Look, Teddy!" Lily woofed delightedly. "Let's go and say hello to that man I saw yesterday. I hope he's got some pie left."

The puppy scooped Teddy up and dashed across the lawn toward the open doors.

Lily was just about to rush up the steps and hurtle into the

house when she heard voices. She
stopped and listened curiously.

"Grandpa, have you found
William yet?"

It was a little girl speaking.
Lily's ears pricked up. Who was
William?

"No, dear, I'm afraid I haven't,"
a man's voice replied.

Lily wondered if it was the old
man she'd seen watching TV the
day before.

"But he must be *somewhere*,
Grandpa." The little girl sounded
as if she were about to cry. Lily felt
very sorry for her. "I know I left
him here the last time I came to
visit."

"Never mind, Amelia," said her

grandpa gently. "I'll buy you a new teddy bear next time we go to town. You can even choose one with a red ribbon, just like William."

"I don't *want* a new teddy bear — I want to find poor William," Amelia howled. She burst into tears.

Lily's ears went down and her tail stopped wagging. She put her teddy bear on the steps and stared sadly at him. "Are *you* William?" she whimpered softly. "Do you belong to Amelia?"

Lily didn't know what to do. She loved her bear very much. But now she'd found out that he belonged to someone else. How would Lily feel if someone took *her* away from Jack and wouldn't give her back?

Lily's ears perked up, and her tail began to wag again. There was only one thing to do.

Chapter Five

Lily picked up the smiling teddy bear and climbed the steps toward the open doors. She could see Amelia sitting on her grandfather's knee, while he wiped her eyes with a big handkerchief. They hadn't noticed the puppy at all.

Lily trotted into the house and laid the teddy bear down on the carpet. "Hello," she woofed. "Don't cry, Amelia — look, I found William for you."

Both Amelia and her grandpa jumped when they heard Lily. They turned around, then looked amazed when they saw a puppy sitting there, next to Amelia's bear.

"It's William!" Amelia gasped, jumping off her gra ndpa's lap.

"And who are *you*?" the old man asked, staring hard at Lily.

"I'm Lily," Lily whimpered. She hoped Amelia and her grandpa wouldn't think that she'd *stolen* William. "I really love Teddy — I mean, William — but he's not mine, so I'm giving him back."

Amelia had grabbed William and was hugging him tightly. "This puppy found William, Grandpa!" she said, her eyes shining. She knelt down and put her arm around Lily. "Isn't she smart?"

"Very smart indeed," her grandfather agreed. Lily's stumpy little tail began to wag again. "I wonder where she found him?"

"William's a little dirty," Amelia said, examining her teddy bear closely. "Maybe he was in the yard."

"He was!" Lily woofed. "I found him under a bush."

"And where have *you* come from?" The old man bent down stiffly and looked at the identity tag on the puppy's collar. "Look, Amelia, her name's Lily. There's a phone number here, too. Maybe we ought to call in case she's lost."

"No, I'm not," Lily barked. "I *never* get lost! Well . . . maybe once or twice . . ."

"Oh, Grandpa, *please*, can we give Lily a treat for finding William?" Amelia begged, her arm still around Lily's neck. "Before you call her owner?"

"A treat!" Lily barked, delighted. She gave Amelia a big wet kiss on her cheek. "Yes, please!"

Amelia and her grandpa took Lily into the kitchen and gave her a bowl of cold chicken. Lily wolfed it down, and then followed it with a very small piece of pie she found on the kitchen floor.

While she was eating, Amelia's grandpa picked up the phone and dialed the number on Lily's collar. "It's busy," he said, putting the phone down. "Never mind, I'll try again soon."

"Grandpa, may I go into the yard and play with Lily?" Amelia asked. She was still clutching William tightly.

Her grandpa nodded. "But maybe you ought to give William to me so that I can wash him," he said with a frown. "He'll be dry by the time your mom comes to pick you up."

"Oh, no, Grandpa," Amelia said quickly. "William's fine!" And she dashed off into the yard with Lily at her heels.

"Why do grown-ups always want to *wash* everything, Lily?" Amelia said with a huge sigh as they ran out onto the lawn.

"I don't know. I don't understand it, either," Lily woofed. She was still feeling kind of sorry that she'd had to give Teddy back, but Amelia looked so happy that Lily knew she'd done the right thing. "Come on, let's chase each other up and down the lawn really fast."

Meanwhile, over at the Harpers' house, Jack had finished his breakfast and watched his favorite cartoon. Now he was ready to take Lily for her walk. He took a quick look around his house, but he couldn't find the puppy anywhere.

He went to ask his mom and dad if they'd seen Lily, but

Mr. Harper had run out to buy a newspaper, and Mrs. Harper was on the phone with Jack's grandma.

"Lily must be in the yard," Jack said to himself, heading for the back door.

Although there was no sign of Lily when he went outside, Jack didn't feel too worried. There were plenty of places in the yard for a small puppy to hide. "Lily!" he called. "Time for your walk!"

He waited. The word *walk* was usually enough to bring Lily running from wherever she was. But this time, she didn't appear.

"Lily?" Jack tried again. But still nothing. No brown-and-white bundle rushing toward him, panting and wagging her tail.

Jack began to feel worried. He knew that his mom and dad had made sure there was no way for the puppy to get out of the yard and wander off. So where on earth could she be? *Surely* she couldn't have gotten out of the yard after all?

His heart pounding with fear, Jack cupped his hands to his mouth. "LILY!" he yelled as loudly as he could.

Was he imagining it, or was that a bark he'd heard? Jack listened hard. There it was again, and it seemed to be coming from the far end of the yard.

Jack raced down the lawn, expecting to see Lily come dashing out of the thick undergrowth toward him. There was still no sign of the puppy, but the barking was getting louder.

Jack pushed his way between the large bushes that stood in front of the fence. "Lily, is that you?" he shouted.

There was another bark, and then a small voice said, "Hello?"

Jack jumped. "Hello," he called. "Who are *you*?"

"I'm Amelia," the girl called back. "Is this your puppy? Her name's Lily."

"Lily's there with *you*?" Jack said, amazed. "In your yard?"

"It's not my yard, it's my grandpa's," Amelia explained.

"But how did Lily get in there?" Jack asked, puzzled.

"I think there's a hole in the fence," Amelia called back. "Lily came in and found my teddy bear, William. I lost him last week."

"So that was *your* bear!" Jack exclaimed.

"Yes, and Lily gave him back to me," Amelia went on. "She's a really smart puppy."

"I know," Jack said proudly. Just then, there was a rustling in the bushes in front of him.

A moment later, Lily appeared with leaves and twigs stuck all over her. She jumped happily into Jack's arms.

"Lily!" Jack cried, giving her a big hug. "I thought you were lost again!"

"Of *course* I wasn't lost,"
Lily woofed, licking Jack's
nose. "I was just taking
William back to his real owner,
that's all!"

Chapter Six

Jack rushed back into the house with Lily, to explain to his mom what had happened.

Mrs. Harper was just saying good-bye to Jack's grandma. But before Jack could say anything, the phone rang again.

It was Mr. Roberts. Amelia had

rushed in to explain everything to her grandpa, too. Mr. Roberts invited Lily, Jack, and Mrs. Harper to drop in and say hello. Lily was delighted.

"Hello, come on in." Amelia's grandfather opened the front door wide, beaming at Mrs. Harper, Jack, and Lily. "I'm Gerry Roberts, and this is my grandaughter, Amelia. Hello again, Lily!"

"Hi!" Lily barked. She rushed over to Amelia, who had William in her arms.

Amelia bent down and gave Lily a cuddle, and Lily gave William a friendly lick.

"Pleased to meet you," said Mrs. Harper, shaking hands with

Mr. Roberts. "We're so glad that Amelia's got her teddy bear back."

"Thanks to Lily," Amelia added gratefully, and Lily gave her a wet kiss on the nose.

"Come and have a snack," Amelia's grandpa said, leading the way into the living room.

Lily's tail began to wag like crazy when she saw plates of cakes and cookies laid out on the table.

"I hope you weren't too worried when you saw that Lily was missing, Jack," said Mr. Roberts.

"I was a *little* worried," Jack admitted with a grin. "You see, Lily's gotten lost before."

"But I always come back!" Lily yapped, eyeing a plate of chocolate cookies.

"Well, we're very grateful to Lily," Mr. Roberts went on. "We've been looking for William all week. Amelia was very upset. She's got lots of other teddy bears, but William's her favorite."

"Grandpa." Amelia pulled at her grandpa's sleeve. "Can I give Lily her present now?"

"Present?" Lily's ears perked up when she heard that. She *loved* presents. "What is it?" she barked.

Mr. Roberts nodded, and Amelia dashed out of the room.

When she came back a moment later, she had a small blue teddy bear in her arms. "This is for you, Lily," she said, holding it out. "His name's Thomas."

Lily could hardly believe her eyes. She went over and sniffed the bear, then gave him a friendly lick. "A teddy bear of my own!" she woofed, thrilled to pieces.

She gently took Thomas from Amelia's hand and showed him proudly to Jack.

"Maybe Amelia and William can come over and play with Thomas and Lily sometimes," Jack suggested. Lily looked from Jack to Mr. Roberts.

"Well, I often look after Amelia while her mother's at work," Mr. Roberts explained. "So maybe Amelia could come over to see Lily when she gets home from school?"

"I think Lily would really love that," Jack agreed.

Lily couldn't say anything, of course, because she was holding Thomas in her mouth, so she just wagged her tail as hard as she could. Now she had *four* new friends: William, Amelia, Mr. Roberts — and Thomas!

DANA

2331 3540